Johnny Delgado:
Private Detective

by

Kevin Brooks

First published in 2006 in Great Britain by
Barrington Stoke Ltd
18 Walker St, Edinburgh EH3 7LP

www.barringtonstoke.co.uk

Reprinted 2006, 2007

ISBN: 978-1-84299-357-6

Printed in Great Britain by Bell & Bain Ltd

A Note from the Author

I started reading detective stories when I was about 11 or 12 years old, and I've gone on reading them ever since. My bookshelves are full of them – I just can't get enough!

One of my favourite crime writers is an American author called Raymond Chandler. He was one of the first people to write detective stories that were based in a world of mean streets and nasty people, a world of violence and corruption. It was a world that his readers could recognise, a world which is like the one that most of us live in.

Chandler was also one of the first authors to write about the kind of detective that we all know and love today. A detective who works on his own, the lone hero, the little guy, the person who looks for the truth. He's someone who can walk the mean streets, but who isn't mean himself.

I've always wanted to write a detective story with these simple ideas in it. With *Johnny Delgado,* I've finally done it. I *loved* writing this book. I hope you enjoy reading it.

This one's for you, Mum

Contents

Chapter 1

The Most Beautiful Girls in the World

It all began with a bit of a problem. It was Friday evening, about six o'clock, and I was sitting by the desk in my bedroom. My bedroom's small, and the flat's small too. It's on the 17th floor of a South London tower block. Rain was drizzling on the window, and the air inside felt hot and steamy.

But that wasn't the problem.

The problem was this. The Most Beautiful Girl in the World was sitting on my bed, and The Second Most Beautiful Girl in the World was sitting next to her. And they were both wearing very tight clothes.

That was the problem.

Their names were Carly (Most Beautiful) and Bex (Second Most Beautiful). They'd been sitting on my bed for the last 20 minutes or so. They were telling me about a kid called Lee Kirk. I *think* that's what they'd been telling me about. It was hard to concentrate with The Two Most Beautiful Girls in the World sitting on my bed.

"So," Carly said to me, "what do you think?"

"Uh?" I said back.

"What do you *think*?" she said. "Do you want the job or not?"

"What job?"

She shook her head. "We just *told* you. What's the *matter* with you? We told you all about it five *minutes* ago."

That's how she talked – sneering all the time, as if everything she talked about was stupid. And when she sneered, her lip curled up at the corner. Somehow that made her seem even more beautiful.

"What are you looking at?" she sneered at me.

"Nothing," I said, "I'm sorry. I was just—"

"What?" said Bex. "You was just *what*?"

I didn't know what to say to that, so I just sat there and stared back at my desk. The thing is, I knew they weren't *really* The Most Beautiful Girls in the World, but girls didn't come into my bedroom that often ... if you know what I mean. It made me feel weird and confused.

Carly was about 17, I'd guess. She was tall and slim, with glossy brown hair and stunning blue eyes. She had that look about her ... you know, the kind of look that makes you feel wobbly and stupid. Bex was younger, about the same age as me – around 15. She was short and blonde, with big full lips and curves everywhere. They both had lots of make-up on, and they were both chewing gum, loudly. And, like I said, they were both sitting on my bed in *very* tight T-shirts and jeans.

"Listen," said Carly with a sigh, "all I want you to do is find out if Lee's seeing this girl."

"What girl?" I said.

"The girl I just *told* you about."

"Oh, yeah ... right. And Lee's your boyfriend?"

"Yeah," Carly said, "he's my *boyfriend*."

"Lee Kirk."

"Yeah, Lee Kirk. I want you to follow him tomorrow night and see where he goes." Carly took a photo out of her pocket and passed it to me. "That's him," she said, "in the photo. And I've put his address on the back. He lives in the West Tower. Fourteenth floor."

The photo was of a hard-looking mug with small dark eyes and scratty blond hair. I'd seen him around the estate. I knew who he was.

"I'll be with him till seven," Carly told me, "and then he's supposed to be going out with his mates."

"But you think he's seeing this girl?"

"Yeah – she's an ugly little bitch called Tanya Nicols. She lives in the West Tower, too. On the second floor. I want you to wait for Lee on the 14th, then follow him down and see where he goes. If he goes into her flat, wait around and see how long he stays. If they go out, follow them." She sniffed, snapped her chewing-gum, then wiped her nose with the back of her hand. She gave me a look. "Do you think you can handle that?"

"Yeah," I said, "I think so."

"Good." She put her hand into her jeans pocket again. This time she pulled out a handful of cash. "How much d'you charge?"

Another problem. For some time now, I'd been putting the word out around the estate that people could hire me as a private detective. Yeah, I know it sounds weird. I'll tell you more about why and all that later on. Right now I want to tell you about this next problem. The problem was this. So far, no-one *had* hired me. So I hadn't really thought about how much money to charge people for what I did. But I didn't want Carly and Bex to know that, did I? I had to think pretty quickly. How much should I charge?

"Well," I said, "it depends ..."

"On what?" said Carly.

"I don't know. How long do you think it'll take?"

Carly shook her head and looked over at Bex. They both smirked at each other, like they *knew* I was just making it up.

"What's the *most* it's going to cost?" said Carly.

"I don't know ..."

"Say it takes you five hours."

"Five hours?" I asked.

"Yeah – seven till twelve. You follow Lee for five hours. How much d'you think that'll cost?"

I had to stop hesitating. So I just picked a figure out of thin air. "Fifty quid?" I said. Carly nodded. She counted out some notes and passed them to Bex.

Bex got up and came over to me. I couldn't help watching the way that she walked – wiggling hips, wiggling curves, wiggling everything. She wiggled right up to me and dropped the money on the desk beside me. Then she put her hands on her hips and just stood there staring at me. Big full lips, lots of curves.

"Where's the bathroom?" she said, and she looked at Carly.

"Uh?"

"The *bathroom*. Where is it?"

My face went red. "Uh … just down the hall," I told her. "On the left."

She grinned at me, then turned round and wiggled her way across the room and out the door.

I looked over at Carly.

She was grinning at me.

I smiled at her.

Her grin vanished.

"What you looking at?" she said.

I shook my head. "Nothing."

Chapter 2
Stupid

After Carly and Bex had left, I stayed in my bedroom for a while and thought about what I'd just done. *What had I done?* Well, I'd got myself a job, my first *paying* job. I'd just earned myself £50 for a few hours' work on a Saturday night. *That's* what I'd done. But did I feel good? No, I didn't. I didn't feel good at all. Because, basically, what I'd just done was plain stupid.

I hadn't thought things through.

I'd been too busy thinking about other things – tight clothes, curves, trying to look cool.

And, worst of all, I'd broken my rules.

You see, when I first decided to become a private detective, I set myself three simple rules.

Rule One. Never get involved with relationship problems.

Rule Two. Never get involved with the local gangs.

Rule Three. Never get involved with the police.

They weren't difficult rules, and they made good sense. Relationship problems are tricky. The gangs are dangerous. And the police ... well, if you get involved with the police around here, you're just asking for trouble.

So, if I stuck to the rules, I had no worries. No danger, no trouble.

Nice and simple.

Right?

Yeah, right. So what do I do when I get my very first job? What do I do? I break at least two of the rules, that's what I do.

Stupid stupid stupid.

I'd just said I'd follow someone who was most likely cheating on his girlfriend.

Stupid.

This someone was a kid called Lee Kirk. And Lee Kirk was a big name in one of the local gangs.

Stupid.

And if he spotted me following him, there was a good chance he'd beat the crap out of me. Then the police would start asking questions.

Stupid.

Yeah, so I felt pretty stupid. But that was nothing to how bad I was going to feel later on, when I found out what was *really* happening.

I was still in my bedroom when Mum came home. It was about seven o'clock. I wasn't doing anything special – just standing at the window, looking out at the rain. Right across from our tower block I could see the other two tower blocks on the estate – the East Tower and the West Tower. Grey concrete, grey glass, grey everything. I scanned the rows of windows. Was there anything happening in the other two tower blocks? All I could see were the dull reflections of the clouded sky in the glass.

I looked down.

Seventeen floors below, the estate was cold and empty in the rain. There wasn't much to see. A couple of cars parked at the back of the lock-up garages. Some kids from the East Tower slouching along Newton Lane. A skinny Alsatian dog skulking around the benches.

My door opened, and I turned round.

"Hey, you," said Mum. "How's it going?"

"OK."

She smiled. "What are you doing?"

"Nothing. How was work?"

She shrugged. "Boring."

Mum has two jobs. She works part-time at the local library, which she likes, and she works part-time at the check-out at Tescos, which she hates. Today was a Tescos day.

She took her hands out of her pockets, crossed her arms, and leaned against the doorway. Her bracelets jangled on her wrists.

"What are you doing tonight?" I asked her.

"Not much. How about you?"

A train juddered along the tracks at the far end of the estate. The bedroom window rattled in its frame.

"I've got homework," I said.

Mum nodded. "I just saw Della's mum in the lift. She said you hadn't been round for a while."

"Right."

Mum smiled. "Della could do with some company."

This was Della Hood she was talking about. Della lived on the same floor as us. She was a year younger than me. She had something wrong with her heart.

15

"She likes you," Mum said.

I shrugged. I felt a bit embarrassed.

Mum smiled again. "Well, it's up to you. Homework or a pretty young girl? I know which one I'd choose."

"Yeah, well," I muttered, "I'll think about it."

"Have you had anything to eat yet?"

"No."

"Let me get changed," she said, "then I'll make us something – OK?"

I smiled at her.

She nodded, looked at me for a moment, then left.

She's half-Mexican, my mum. She was born in a little farming village in the north of Mexico. She came to England when she was a baby with *her* mum. Just the two of them together. My mum never knew who her father was.

But I know who my father was. His name was David Cherry. He was a policeman, a detective, an officer in the CID. He met my mum about 16 years ago when she was working as a dancer in a nightclub. He was already married. But he fell in love with my mum. They had an affair. And then along came me.

The affair didn't last long. And Dad never left his wife, but he always kept in touch with us. He was great – kind and cool, really funny, but sort of sad, too. I liked him a lot.

Five years ago he was killed in a drug raid.

No-one was ever charged or arrested for his murder. The killer was never found.

Maybe that's why I want to be a private detective. Maybe I want to be like my dad. Or maybe I want to find out who killed him.

Maybe I just thought it was better than doing a paper round.

Who knows?

I really miss my dad.

Chapter 3
Marcus and Della

After Mum and I had had something to eat, I went to see Della. I wasn't really sure if I *wanted* to see her. But I didn't want to spend all night staring at history books either. I said goodbye to Mum and walked along to Della's flat. I was feeling a bit nervous. Della always made me feel like that. I knew that she liked me, and – to be honest – I quite liked her. But what was a bit difficult was that I didn't really know *how* I liked her.

Was she a friend? A good friend? Or did I like her a bit *more* than just as a friend?

I didn't know.

I got to her door and rang the bell. As I waited, I started to see her face in my mind. She had curly blonde hair, sparkling blue eyes, and a brace on her teeth. In my head I could see that funny little smile – and when I heard the sound of footsteps coming towards the door, my heart started thumping. But when the door opened, it wasn't Della that I saw, but her older brother, Marcus.

"Hey, Delgado," he said with a big grin. "What's happening?"

"Oh, right ... hi, Marcus. I was looking for Della."

"She's out," he said. "Gone to see the ticker man."

I didn't know what he meant, so I just went on looking at him. He didn't have a shirt on, just big baggy combats and a string of gold chains around his neck. A tufty little beard sprouted from his chin.

"Della's heart," Marcus said, and he gave his chest a slap. "Playing her up a bit today."

"Oh," I said.

I got it now. Della had gone to see her doctor, something to do with her heart.

"Hey, it's cool," Marcus grinned. "She'll be back."

"Right."

"You wanna wait?"

"OK."

And that's how I ended up talking to Marcus about Lee Kirk.

Marcus Hood knows everything there is to know about the estate. He knows all the names and faces, all the gangs, all the goings-on. He knows who's coming up, and who's going down, and who's getting out. He knows who's robbing who, and who's selling what, and who's going to get it. He knows what's going down before it goes down, and he knows what that means. He knows the lot, basically.

But the funny thing is – no-one seems to know anything about him. Even though he *knows* everyone, he doesn't seem to have any friends. He knows everyone's phone number, but no-one knows his. He doesn't work, but he's always got plenty of money. And that usually means drugs. But Marcus doesn't do drugs, and he certainly doesn't sell drugs, but he knows all the gangs and the dealers.

It's kind of odd.

There are rumours, of course. Whispers. I've heard the word *grass* once or twice when people have been talking about Marcus, but no-one's ever had any proof. And no-one's got the guts to find out. It's not worth it.

Marcus isn't that hard himself, but he knows a lot of heavy people. And he's owed a lot of favours. So everyone leaves him alone.

Personally, it's never bothered *me* what Marcus does. As long as he's OK with me, why should I care what he does?

And he *was* OK with me.

That evening, he showed me into the front room, sat me down, and asked if I wanted a cup of tea. It might not sound like much, but I didn't expect him to do that for me, and it made me feel pretty good.

While he was in the kitchen, I had a quick look around the flat. It was exactly the same as mine – same layout, same size, same everything. The only difference was, it was a lot messier. It wasn't dirty or anything, but the whole place was jam-packed with stuff. Everywhere I looked, there were boxes and bags full of all kinds of stuff – computer games, DVDs, CDs, hair-dryers, boxes of perfume and aftershave, piles of brand new clothes. There was even a big cardboard box full of Harry Potter figures sitting on the top of the TV.

Marcus came back in, handed me a mug of tea, then sat down cross-legged on the floor. He'd put a hoodie on. The zip was undone, but the hood was up. He lit a cigarette.

"I hear you've been talking to Carly," he said.

"What?"

"Carly and Bex." He winked at me. "Nice girls."

"Oh, yeah ... right."

He grinned. "You're really doing this P.I. thing then?"

"Sorry?" I asked. I didn't understand.

"P.I. ... private investigator ... private detective ... whatever ... you're really doing it?"

"Yeah, I suppose ..."

He gulped some tea. "Toog told me you found his cat."

I smiled. Marcus was talking about Benny Toogood. Everyone calls him Toog. He's a strange man – six foot six and a real giant. He's got a huge square head and hands like shovels. He's also kind of slow, and not too smart. He's not backward or anything, just very ... *very* ... slow. A few weeks ago, I'd bumped into him in the lift. He was crying. He'd lost his cat, he told me, and he really *loved* his cat. So I helped him to look for it. And I found it. It was at the vet's. Toog had taken it in that morning to get its nails clipped, and then he'd simply forgotten all about it.

"You're his hero," Marcus told me. "Toog thinks you're a genius."

"Toog's all right," I said.

"Yeah," Marcus agreed. "He's cool." He took a long drag on his cigarette. Then he looked at me. "You never know when you might need someone like Toog," he said. "It's always good to have someone looking out for you." He tapped his cigarette into an ashtray. "Most of all if you're stupid enough to get mixed up with people like Lee Kirk." He looked at me again. "You know who he is, don't you?" he asked.

I shrugged. "Sort of ..."

Marcus shook his head. "He's The Man, that's who he is. Or he soon will be."

For the next ten minutes, Marcus told me all about Lee Kirk. He told me how he'd worked himself up from being a simple gang member to being second-in-command of the

Westies, the gang who run the West Tower, and that he was now getting ready to take out the current boss, a kid called Tyrell Jones, and then take control of the Westies himself. After that, he planned to join up with the other local gang, the E Boys, and take over the whole estate.

"Kirk's a psycho," Marcus told me. "But he's clever, too. Very clever. He knows how it works, all the gang stuff – the rules, the drugs, the guns. He knows how to play it. Do you know what I mean?"

"Not really," I said.

Marcus laughed. "Yeah, well, that's good. Keep it that way and you'll be all right. Don't get sucked into it, man. The whole gang thing is a load of shit. It's a cop-out. They think it's all about power and money, which it is, but they don't *use* it for anything. They just hang around, wasting time, talking shit, waiting for something to happen." He looked at me. "But listen – Kirk's different. He's ambitious. He's going places. And if anyone gets in his way, he won't think twice about taking him out. So, be careful – OK?"

"I'm only going to follow him. He won't even know I'm there."

Marcus shook his head. "He'll know."

"Yeah, well ..."

Marcus shrugged. "It's up to you. I'm just letting you know, that's all."

"Yeah ... thanks."

The room went quiet for a while, and everything felt kind of edgy. Marcus kept looking right at me for a moment. He gave me a long, hard look. Then slowly, and without a smile, he finished drinking his tea and stood up. He scratched his belly, yawned, then grinned at me.

"All right?"

"Yeah."

"OK."

With that, Marcus strode over to the TV and cracked open the big cardboard box that was sitting on the top. The next thing I knew, Marcus was offering me a Harry Potter figure in a plastic box.

"You want a Hagrid?" he said

"That's Snape," I told him.

He shrugged. "Whatever – you want it?"

"No, thanks."

"Suit yourself."

Just then, the door opened and Della came in with her mum. Della didn't look very well. Her face was pale and tired, and there was a small Band-Aid on her neck. Her mum was carrying a big bottle of pills and an oxygen mask.

I stood up.

Della smiled at me. "Hello, Johnny."

"Hey," I said. "How's it going?"

"I'm all right. I was just—"

"Della," her mum cut in, "you get off to bed now."

"Can't I just—?"

"Not now." Mrs Hood looked at me, then back at Della. "You can see Johnny some other time. Right now you need to get some rest. Go on."

Della gave me an awkward smile. I smiled back at her. She gave me a little wave, then turned round and went off to her room. I looked quickly over at Mrs Hood. She looked worried. I looked down. I felt a bit embarrassed. Like I was an intruder or something.

"I'd better go," I mumbled.

Mrs Hood just nodded silently and went into the kitchen. I watched her go. She looked sad and very tired. The sadness seemed to stay in the air behind her like a poisonous cloud.

Marcus stood up and put his hand on my shoulder. "Hey, don't worry about it," he told me. "Mum just gets worked up about things. Next time you see her she'll be fine."

I looked at him.

He smiled. "Don't *worry*. I'll tell Della you'll call her in a couple of days. She'll be fine by then. OK?"

"Yeah, OK," I said.

"Right," he grinned, "go on then, piss off home. I got stuff to do." He patted me on the shoulder. "And don't forget what I said about Kirk. Just watch yourself – OK?"

Chapter 4
Thinking and Waiting

I spent most of Saturday just hanging around the flat doing nothing. Mum was working at the library today. And I was on my own.

So I was thinking.

Mostly, I was thinking about Lee Kirk. I kept looking at his photo, the one that Carly had given me. And every time I looked at it, I thought about what Marcus had said. *He's a psycho ... he's clever ... he's different ...*

be careful. The more I thought about it, the more I wanted to get in touch with Carly and tell her I'd changed my mind. I didn't want to go snooping around after a psycho. It was stupid. Dangerous. Scary. But I'd said I'd do it, hadn't I? I'd taken the money. And if I *really* wanted to be a private detective, I couldn't change my mind about a job just because I'd got a bit scared, could I?

That wouldn't be right.

I'd said I'd do it, so I'd do it.

Anyway, I didn't know how to get in touch with Carly. I hadn't got her address or phone number. She'd said *she* would phone *me* to see what I'd found out.

Stupid.

At six-thirty that evening, just after Mum got home, I put on my coat, picked up my phone, and got ready to leave.

"Going out?" said Mum.

33

"Yeah, I won't be long."

"Where are you going?"

"Steve's place."

"Steve who?"

"Steve Devine. You know, from school? He lives in the West Tower."

Mum shrugged, as if she'd never heard of Steve Devine. That wasn't surprising. I'd just made him up.

"All right," she said. "Well, mind how you go. And don't be too late."

****

There are three tower blocks on the estate – the North Tower (mine), the West Tower, and the East Tower. Each of them has 23 floors, and each of the floors has ten flats. Two hundred and thirty flats to a block, nearly seven hundred flats in all. That's a lot of flats, a lot of people. Each of the floors in each of the blocks is exactly the same. There's a corridor on each floor with a row of flats on both sides. There's a lift at one end of the corridor and stairs at the other. The doors to the stairwells are dirty yellow. The walls are painted a horrible sickly green, and the floors are covered with some kind of dirty brown plasticky stuff. There are lights in the ceiling, a couple of windows at the end of each corridor, and that's about it.

There was no-one around when I left my flat. The corridor was empty, the lift was empty. When I got out downstairs, there was no-one there either.

I headed off across towards the West Tower. The space in between the towers is called "the square"... I don't know why it's called that. It *isn't* a square. It's just a rough patch of tarmac with a few crappy benches and a road at one end. It's not even a square *shape*.

The road goes in between the North Tower and the other two towers and I headed across it. The evening light was beginning to dim, and a fine rain was falling. I could hear loud music blaring out from a flat somewhere, but there were hardly any people around. A homeless old guy was digging through the bins by the benches, and there were a couple of E Boys hanging around on the other side of the road, but that was about it.

I crossed the road and hurried over to the West Tower. It was getting cold now. The clouds were low and heavy, and an icy wind was whipping around the estate, blowing rain into my face. In the cold shadows of the tower blocks, everything looked dark and gloomy.

I gazed up. The West Tower was in front of me, the East was to my left, and the North was behind me. Three great blocks of dirty grey concrete, seven hundred poky little flats, two thousand or so people.

It's a world within a world.

****

As I came up to the entrance of the West Tower, I saw a few younger kids hanging around the doors. Most of them were on bikes, and most of them had mobile phones. They were runners. Delivery boys. Look-outs. Working for the Westies. The oldest of them was about 12 years old. They watched me as I went through the doors and into the downstairs lobby. One of them came over and stood next to me as I pressed the button for the lift. He had chains around his neck and a snotty nose.

When the lift came down, the snotty kid got in with me.

"What floor d'you want?" he said.

"Thirteen," I lied.

He hit the buttons – 13 and 18.

The doors closed and the lift started moving. I looked at the kid. He stared at the phone in his hand. It was a top-of-the-range Nokia – camera, 3G, movies, everything.

When the lift stopped at 13 and I stepped out, I saw the kid put the phone to his ear and start talking. I waited for the doors to close, then I went down the corridor and walked up the stairs to the 14th. I didn't open the stairwell doors and go into the corridor yet.

It was five to seven.

I stood in the stairwell and waited.

Chapter 5
Everything Goes Black

From where I was standing, I couldn't see the door to Lee Kirk's flat, but I thought I'd hear him when he came out. And I was right. Bang on seven o'clock, I heard a door open, and when I opened the stairwell door and stepped out into the corridor, there he was – Lee Kirk. Coming out of his flat. His blond hair was all gelled up, and he was wearing black track pants and a white Nike hoodie.

He wasn't very big, but he looked a lot nastier than his photograph. Nasty and cold and hard.

My heart was pounding as I walked along the corridor towards him. I pulled a piece of paper from my pocket and pretended to read it. Earlier, I'd written a name and address on the paper, a made-up name and address – *Barry Jennings, Flat 1604, West Tower, William B. Foster Estate.* The idea was that if anyone asked me what I was doing here, I could pretend I was lost. I was just some dopey kid, looking for someone called Barry Jennings. It wasn't much of an idea, but it was better than nothing.

And Lee Kirk wasn't even looking at me anyway. As I walked passed him, frowning at my piece of paper, he was too busy locking his door and sorting out his phone and stuff to notice me.

So far, so good.

40

I carried on down to the end of the corridor and stopped by the lift. I waited, pretending to study my piece of paper again. When I heard Kirk's footsteps coming up behind me, I hit the button for the lift. The light came on, and I heard the distant whirring and clunking of the lift as it started moving up the shaft.

I could sense Kirk standing behind me now. I could smell his aftershave. I could feel his presence. It didn't feel good. I forced myself to stay calm. *Don't move, don't turn round, don't look at him.*

The lift seemed to take an age.

I was beginning to sweat.

My legs felt shaky.

The silence was killing me.

I wanted to turn round and say – *Hi, I'm not following you, you know. Honestly. I'm not doing anything. I'm just waiting for the lift ...*

But I forced myself not to.

In the end, after the longest 30 seconds of my life, I heard a dull-sounding *ting*, and then a juddering *clunk* as the lift finally arrived. I stared at the doors, waiting for them to open.

And when they did, that's when everything went wrong.

There were two of them in the lift. A tall black kid in wrap-around shades, and an ugly-looking guy with a face like a pizza. The pizza-faced guy had a bottle in his hand. They were both staring at me.

I didn't even have time to step back. As soon as the doors opened, Kirk grabbed me from behind and shoved me into the lift, and before I knew what was happening, someone hit me hard in the belly and I fell to the floor, gasping for breath.

"Doors," I heard someone say.

A button thumped, and I heard the doors closing. As the lift started moving, I tried to get to my feet, but I didn't have a chance. The first kick slammed me back to the floor, the second one got me in the belly again, and the third one made everything go black.

Chapter 6
The Fall

I'm floating in space. Everything's dark. Stars are spinning faintly in the distance. There are planets, big square planets. Square and flat, like walls. Silver walls. Wooden walls. They keep drifting towards me, knocking into my head, then bouncing away. They're ships. I'm drowning. I'm drinking the sea. It tastes sweet. Sweet and strong. Sour and fruity. It's black ...

Everything's black.

Everything's gone.

****

When I woke up, the first thing I saw was that I was holding a knife. A big, heavy knife. The silver blade was sticky with blood. My hand was red, too. I opened my fingers and the knife fell to the floor.

The floor was grey. A grey carpet.

My head hurt.

My belly hurt.

I felt sick.

I couldn't remember anything.

I closed my eyes and tried to think – *Where am I? What happened to me? Where did the knife come from? Why is it covered in blood?*

Nothing. No answers. My mind was empty. I could remember Kirk shoving me into the lift, then someone kicking me in the head ... but that was it. After that – nothing.

I opened my eyes and looked around.

I was lying on a grubby settee in the front room of a dim and shadowy flat. The curtains were shut. It was dark outside. Night-time. Late. The TV was on, Match of the Day, the sound turned off. The room was a mess – unwashed plates on the table, dirty clothes on the floor, rubbish all over the place. The air smelled stale. The flat felt empty and quiet, but I could hear dim sounds from somewhere else – rap music, voices shouting, a police car wailing in the distance ...

The sounds of the estate.

I'm still on the estate, I thought. *I'm in a flat, somewhere on the estate.*

It didn't make me feel much better, but at least it was something. I felt in my pocket for my phone, but it wasn't there. I searched all my other pockets – nothing. I started to sit up, groaning at the pain in my belly ... and that's when I saw him.

He was lying on the floor by the window. Face up, his eyes wide open, staring at nothing. He was covered in blood.

It was Tyrell Jones, the leader of the Westies.

I knew he was dead, but I still had to check. My legs felt wobbly as I went over and crouched down beside him. When I saw all the blood, I thought I was going to be sick. He'd been stabbed in the chest and the stomach. I could see the stab wounds through his shirt – deep and ugly, thick with blood. There were at least three of them, maybe more. His hands were cut, too. And his face was all battered and smashed.

I put my fingers on his neck and felt for his pulse, but there was nothing.

He wasn't breathing.

His skin was cold.

He was dead.

Stabbed ...

I looked down at the blood on my hands. There was blood on my shirt, too. But I wasn't hurt. It wasn't my blood. My heart sank as I looked over at the knife I'd dropped on the floor ... the knife I'd had in my hand when I woke up.

The knife ...

I looked back at Tyrell's body again. The stab wounds in his chest ...

Then I looked at the knife.

The stab wounds.

The knife.

Oh, God ... had *I* killed him?

Had I stabbed Tyrell Jones to death?

****

My head was spinning now. I was trying to think, trying to remember, trying to stay calm. But I couldn't. Couldn't think. Couldn't remember. Couldn't stay calm.

I couldn't do anything. All I could do was stare at the blood on my hands.

Then I heard it again – the police siren. It was closer now. A *lot* closer. I got to my feet fast and went over to the window. I heard the sound of tyres squealing outside, and when I pulled back the curtain I saw the flashing lights of two patrol cars swerving off the road and speeding into the estate.

I closed the curtain.

Which tower was I in?

Breathing fast, I opened the curtain again, took a quick look around outside, then shut it again.

I was in the West Tower. Third or fourth floor.

I was in a lot of trouble.

I was trapped in a room with a dead body. I had blood on my hands, and my fingerprints were all over the murder weapon. The police would be here any minute, and I couldn't explain anything. I didn't even know how I'd got here.

I had to get out.

I tried the front door, but it was locked. No key. I ran back into the front room and looked out of the window again. The police cars were parked down below. Their doors were shut but the lights were still flashing. Kids from the estate were beginning to crowd the cars, laughing and shouting. I guessed the policemen must be on their way up now. Some in the lift, some on the stairs. Covering all exits.

I leaned out of the window now and looked straight down. I could see the window of the flat below. It was open. Could I get down there? The outside wall was smooth, but half-way down, between me and the flat below, there was a ventilator shaft. If I could just get a foothold on that ...

I didn't have time to think. I could hear running footsteps in the corridor now. Voices. Police radios. I opened the window and crawled out onto the sill ...

Fists started hammering on the door.

I grabbed hold of the window sill and let my legs slide down ...

Shouts – "Police! Open up! Open the door!"

My feet couldn't find the ventilator shaft. I was hanging on the sill, three floors up, waving my feet around in the air ...

THUMP! The front door of the flat cracked and splintered. They'd kicked it in ... I took a deep breath, closed my eyes, and let go of the ledge. For a terrifying instant, I just fell – my heart frozen, my hands scrabbling madly at the wall – and then my feet hit the ventilator shaft. I felt it crack, then my feet started to slip off, and for a moment I was falling again. Somehow I grabbed hold of a bit of the ventilator shaft as I fell, and at the same time my feet struck the window ledge of the flat below. The next thing I knew I was scrambling in through the open window and dropping down onto the floor.

Above me, I could hear a door smash open and heavy boots crashing into the room.

I shut the window and breathed out hard.

I was shaking like a wreck.

Chapter 7
Madness and Goodness

"Can I help you?"

The voice came from the middle of the room behind me. I spun round and saw a mad-looking old woman standing there. My mouth dropped open. I'd totally forgotten that someone might *live* in the flat I'd come to. I was too shocked to speak. I just stood there and stared, and the woman stared back at me.

She was about a million years old. Her hair was wild and grey, like a mad bird's nest, and her wrinkly old face was covered in make-up – purple eyes, jet-black eyebrows, bright pink lips. She was wearing a blue tracksuit, cheap white trainers, and a pair of black lace gloves.

Mad as a bat.

"I know you," she said suddenly.

"Sorry?"

"You're Maria's boy, aren't you? Jimmy Delgado."

"Johnny," I said.

She cupped a hand to her ear. "What?"

"Johnny ... Johnny Delgado."

"That's what I said." She clacked her teeth. "Your mum's a kind lady. She helped me up the stairs once. She told me all about you, said you were a good boy."

"Right ..."

I could hear more sirens now. More police. I could hear them upstairs, in the corridor, knocking on all the other doors.

"Betty Travis," the old woman said.

"What?"

"My name's Betty Travis. I expect your mum told you about me. She helped me up the stairs, you know."

"Yeah ..."

"What have you done?" she said.

"Sorry?"

She stared at me. "I might be a bit mad, young man, but I'm not stupid. You've just climbed through my window. The police are all over the place. You're sweating and shaking and you're covered in blood." She smiled at me. "If you want me to help you, I think you'd better start talking."

55

I thought about running for it, just legging it out of the door, but I knew I wouldn't get very far. Betty was right – I needed help. I didn't know *why* she wanted to help me, and I didn't know *how* she could help me, but there was nothing else I could do.

So I started talking.

When I'd told her everything I could, she didn't say anything for a while, just stared at me.

After what seemed like a long time, she said, "Do you expect me to believe all that?"

I shrugged. "It's the truth."

She looked at me for a moment longer, then nodded. "Right," she said. "The bathroom's down there. Get yourself washed and out of those clothes."

Five minutes later, I was pushing Betty down the corridor to the lift in a wheelchair. My hands were clean, the blood was washed

off, and I had a scratchy blue tracksuit on.
My own bloodstained clothes were tumbling
around in Betty's washing machine.

As we got nearer to the lift, I saw there
were two policeman standing guard beside it.

"Keep your mouth shut," Betty whispered.
"Let me do the talking."

I carried on wheeling her towards the lift.
The two policemen were watching us now. I
tried to look as innocent as possible. I was
just some kid ... a kid with a batty old gran in
a wheelchair. That's all I was.

We were almost at the lift, when suddenly
Betty started to shake her head to and fro
and jabber away like a mad woman. "What's
going on?" she cackled. "What's this?" She
waved her hands at the policemen. "Who are
you? What do you want? I haven't done
anything ... what's going on?"

Both the policemen looked startled. They turned to me.

"Sorry," I said, "she's just a bit—"

"Jimmy?" Betty screeched. "Jimmy ... what's this? What do they want? I haven't done anything ..."

One of the policemen pressed the lift button. The other one tried to smile. It was the kind of smile you give to mad people.

While Betty carried on jabbering and screeching, I smiled back at the policeman. "What's going on?" I asked him in a casual voice. "Has there been some trouble?"

He shrugged. "Nothing to worry about."

I nodded.

Betty lurched forward and swung her arm at him.

I pulled her back into the wheelchair. "Sorry ..."

The lift doors opened, and the policemen moved to one side. I wheeled Betty into the lift and hit the button for the ground floor. Betty kept on with her crazy act until the doors had closed again and the lift had started moving, and then she suddenly stopped.

"All right?" she said calmly and smiled at me.

"Very good," I said. "Very realistic."

She laughed. "I've had a lot of practice."

There were more police downstairs, and more outside the tower block, but none of them bothered us. Maybe the others had radioed down to let them know we were coming. Most of the estate kids hanging around outside were too busy jumping round the patrol cars to notice me, but I saw one or two of them nudge each other and point at me. But no-one said anything.

I wheeled Betty across the road, through the square, and into the North Tower. I couldn't see any policemen around yet, but I was pretty sure they'd be here soon, so I didn't waste any time. Into the lobby, into the lift, shut the doors.

"Tenth floor," Betty said.

"What?"

"I've got a friend on the tenth floor. You can drop me off there."

I hit ten.

The lift started moving.

I looked down at Betty. "Why are you doing this?" I asked her. "Why are you helping me?"

"Your eyes," she said.

"My eyes?"

She smiled at me. "You have good eyes."

Tenth floor. The doors opened and Betty got out. She pushed the wheelchair out in front of her.

"Thank you," I said.

She smiled again. "Come and see me some time. Keep a mad woman company for a while."

"OK," I said.

She put her hand into the pocket of her tracksuit and passed me a mobile phone. "Here, take it. Let your mum know you're all right. You can bring it back when you come round to see me." She leaned back into the lift and pressed the button for the 23rd floor. Then she stepped back. "*Adios*, Johnny," she said.

As the doors shut I stared at her, unable to speak.

How did she know I needed a phone? And how did she know I was going to the 23rd floor?

How did she *know* that? It's not as if it's where I live.

Chapter 8
Secrets and Lies

I've got a secret hiding place.

To get to it, you have to go up to the 23rd floor and follow the corridor right down to the end. Then you go through a door marked – *PRIVATE. NO ENTRY!* The door is always locked, so you need a key. I've had my key for about three years now. I borrowed it from the man from the council. He left the key in the door by mistake. I keep my key hidden away beneath a piece of loose floor near the door.

I go to my secret place when I want to be on my own and think about things. And that night I really needed to be on my own and think about things. There was a lot to think about.

After I'd made sure that no-one was watching me, I got the key from under the flooring, opened the door, then locked it behind me. The door goes into a little room that's filled with all sorts of stuff – cupboards and shelves, boxes of tools, pipes and cables, heating controls. I went across the room and through a little archway. Then I went up some steps to another door. I pushed open that door and stepped out into a breeze of cold night air. I was on the roof of the tower block now. High above the ground. I could see for miles. I could see the lights of houses and blocks of flats, headlights streaming on invisible roads, street lights, traffic lights, the lights of London glowing in the distance ...

But there wasn't time to enjoy the view.

I hurried across the roof, heading towards my secret place.

My secret place is a shed. A metal shed. It has a metal door, metal walls, and a metal roof. Inside, there's a big metal cabinet covered in dials and displays. I'm not sure what it is, but it hums all the time. It's also nice and warm. Apart from the cabinet and a couple of old chairs, the rest of the shed is empty.

Empty and quiet. I shut the door behind me, sat down on one of the chairs, and started to think.

Think.

What's going on?

What happened?

How?

Why?

What are you going to do?

I thought about it. I thought hard, looking for why everything had happened the way it did. Looking for answers. Looking for facts. I tried to remember ... but I still couldn't. My head felt thick and dizzy.

I decided to stick to the facts.

Fact One – Someone had killed Tyrell Jones.

Fact Two – Either that someone was me, or someone else had framed me. They'd made it look as if it was me.

Fact Three – Even if I *could* kill someone, which I didn't think I could, why would I kill Tyrell Jones?

Fact Four – Lee Kirk wanted to kill Tyrell Jones. If Marcus was right, and most of the time he *is* right, Kirk was planning to take over all the gangs on the estate. With Tyrell out of the way, there was nothing to stop him.

Fact Five – Kirk was a psycho.

Fact Six – Kirk was clever.

What did it all add up to? Kirk had set me up. He'd got Carly and Bex to hire me so that I'd follow him. Then he'd got me in the lift, beaten me up and left me in the flat with Tyrell's dead body. Maybe he'd called the police, too. Had he given them my name as well?

Why? So that no-one would know who the real killer was. And the real killer was him. Kirk.

Yeah, but why did Kirk choose me? Why did I have to take the rap?

I didn't know the answer to that. Right now that didn't matter. What was bothering me right now was – what the hell was I going to do?

I called Mum first. I got Betty's mobile out of my pocket, punched in the number, and waited.

"Hello?"

"Mum, it's me—"

"*Hola, Juan. Cómo estás?*"

"What?" I said. "It's me, Mum – Johnny. Why are you speaking Spanish?"

"*Policía,*" she whispered. "*Dónde estás?*"

I got it then. She was speaking Spanish because the police were there. In the flat. She didn't want them to know she was talking to me. She wanted to know where I was.

"*Estoy a salvo,*" I told her. (I'm safe.) "*No he hecho nada.*" (I haven't done anything.)

"*Ya lo sé,*" she said. (I know.) "*No vengas a casa todavía. Llama a Della – OK?*" (Don't come home yet. Call Della – OK?)

"OK," I said.

She put her phone down.

I thought about what she'd just said for a moment, then I called Della.

"Hello?"

"Della – it's Johnny."

"Johnny!" she cried. "What's going on? Are you all right? I was with your mum just now and the police came round. They're looking for you."

"Yeah, I know. I just spoke to Mum on the phone."

"Where are you? All you all right?"

"I'm fine. What did the police say?"

"They wanted to know where you were. They wouldn't say why." She hesitated a moment. "They found the letter, Johnny."

"What letter?"

"It was hidden in the bathroom."

"*What*? What are you *talking* about?"

"One of the policemen went into your bathroom and came back with a letter. I only saw it for a second. It was something to do with your dad."

"My dad?" I couldn't believe it. "A letter about my *dad*?"

"Yeah ... haven't you seen it?"

"I don't know anything about any letter. What did it say?"

Della hesitated again. "It didn't say who it was from ... it wasn't signed ..."

"But what did it *say*, Della?"

"Whoever wrote it ... they said they knew who killed your dad. They named him."

I couldn't speak for a moment. I was too confused. Too shocked.

"Johnny?" said Della. "Are you still there?"

"Who did it?" I said quietly. "Who killed my dad?"

"Someone called Jones," Della said. "Lester Jones."

It was too much. Everything was just too much.

My mind went blank and I stared at the floor.

Lester Jones was Tyrell Jones's father.

Chapter 9
Something and Nothing

"Johnny? Yo, Johnny D! You there? Hey, Delgado? Hey, *HEY* ... speak to me."

The voice on the phone seemed miles away. *I* was miles away. My mind was still blank. I couldn't think.

The voice called out again. "Hey! HEY! *HEY*!"

Still in a daze, I lifted my hand from my lap and put the phone to my ear. "Hello?"

"Delgado? Christ, what are you *doing*? I thought you'd *died* or something."

It was Marcus.

"Sorry ..." I mumbled. "I was just thinking ..."

"You ain't got time to think. You're up to your neck in shit. I *told* you not to go messing with Kirk."

"Yeah ..."

"All right, listen," he said. "You listening?"

"Yeah."

"Right, talk to me. Tell me what happened."

I told Marcus everything. From getting beaten up in the lift, to wheeling Betty Travis out of the West Tower and across to the North, then talking to Mum and Della on the phone. Everything. When I'd finished, Marcus

73

was quiet for a second or two, and I imagined him sitting in his flat with the phone to his ear, thinking hard.

"OK," he said after a while. "I think I get it."

"Kirk set me up," I said.

"Of *course* he did," Marcus said with a sigh. "I knew that before I even spoke to you. I just didn't know how he did it."

"Do you know now?"

"The guy in the lift ... you said he was carrying a bottle?"

"Yeah."

"They drugged you. After they'd beaten you up, they made you drink whatever was in the bottle. It was probably full of Roofies or something."

"What are Roofies?"

"You know, they're the date-rape drug. Roofies make you feel drunk and sleepy, and when you wake up you can't remember anything. They drugged you, killed Tyrell, then left you in his flat with the knife they'd used to murder Tyrell. Then they called the cops."

"What about the letter they found in the bathroom?" I asked him. "I don't understand—"

"It's a fake," he said. "Kirk probably wrote it. Carly and Bex planted it when they were at your place."

"Why?"

"It gives you a reason for killing Tyrell. You get a letter saying his dad killed your dad, you've got a reason to kill him."

"That's *crazy*. I wouldn't—"

"It worked, didn't it?" Marcus said. "The police are looking for you. They're not looking for Kirk, are they?"

He was right, of course. I could see it all now. Marcus was right. He'd been right all along. And I'd been even stupider than I thought.

"Where are you now?" Marcus said.

"On the roof. You go up to the top floor—"

"Yeah, I know how to get there. Are you in the shed?"

"How do *you* know about the shed?"

He laughed. "I know everything."

"Yeah, but—"

"Just stay there, OK? I'll be with you in about 20 minutes."

"What are you going to do?"

"You'll find out when I get there," he said.

76

It was a long 20 minutes. I sat in the shed for a while, just trying to think, but there was too much going on in my head. Too many feelings, too many emotions.

Fear.

Anger.

Shame.

Sadness.

When Della had told me about the letter, I'd felt something stir inside me. The idea that Lester Jones had killed my dad ... well, it was something. Something to hold on to. A name, at last. A suspect. Someone to blame.

But now, now that I knew it wasn't true ...

Now there was nothing again.

I stopped thinking and went out onto the roof.

The night air was really cold now. Cold and fresh and silent. The sky was pitch black, and the world stretched out beneath me. Twenty-three floors below. I stood on the edge of the roof and looked down. In the glow of the flashing blue lights, I could see the dim outline of the square. The lock-up garages. The bins. The benches.

Twenty-three floors below.

It was a long way down.

Chapter 10
How Do You Think It Feels?

When the door to the roof opened, I was surprised to see that Marcus wasn't alone. I was even more surprised when I saw who was with him. As he came through the door, I saw the giant figure of Toog behind him. And behind Toog, being dragged by his hair, was Lee Kirk.

"Hey, Johnny," Marcus said, "how's it going?"

I looked at Toog. He grinned at me. He was dragging Lee Kirk in one huge hand, almost lifting him off his feet. Kirk was squirming and twisting around, gripping Toog's hand to stop his hair being pulled out by the roots. His nose was bleeding and one of his eyes was black and blue and swollen.

The three of them came over to me, and we stood there together at the edge of the roof. I put my hand in my pocket and felt for Betty's phone.

"What's going on?" I asked Marcus.

"Not much," he said. "I just thought it was time we had a little chat with The Man here. You know, get things sorted ..." He glanced at Kirk. "What do you think, Lee? You feel like talking?"

Kirk glared at him. "You're a dead man, Hood. You're finished—"

"Yeah, yeah," Marcus said calmly. "You've already told me all that. It's getting kind of boring. How about telling us something else?"

"Like what?"

"Like how you set Johnny up, for a start."

Kirk spat on the floor, then grinned coldly at me. "How's your head, kid? You look a bit pale." He laughed. "Hey, I hear you found out who killed your old man. Is that right?"

I stared at him.

"Lester Jones, eh?" He laughed again. "Who'd have thought it? I *knew* all those rumours weren't true."

"What rumours?" I said.

Kirk looked at Marcus. "Doesn't he know?"

"Shut up, Kirk," Marcus said.

Kirk ignored him, turning back to me with a grin. "Your old man ... they say he was taken out by another cop. A contract hit." He raised his eyebrows. He thought it was funny that I was so shocked. "Didn't you know? I thought everyone on the estate knew that."

I looked at Marcus. "What's he talking about?"

"Nothing," Marcus said quickly. "Don't listen to him. He's just trying to wind you up." He turned to Kirk, his eyes suddenly hard. "You talk too much."

"Yeah? What are you going to do about it?"

"How about I throw you off the roof?"

Kirk shook his head. "If you think you can scare me—"

"I'm not trying to scare you," Marcus said simply. "I'm just going to kill you." He glanced up at Toog. "Ready?"

Toog nodded.

"Do it," Marcus told him.

Toog raised his hand and started dragging Kirk towards the edge of the roof. For a moment or two, Kirk didn't do anything. He didn't believe they were serious. He thought they were just bluffing. But as Toog dragged him ever closer to the edge, Kirk began to see that maybe they *weren't* bluffing after all, and that's when he started to panic.

"Hey ... hold on," he shouted, "come on, don't be stupid ... no, you can't ... hey, lemme go ..."

He was digging his heels in now, struggling hard. His eyes were white with fear as he tried to free himself from Toog's giant hand. But Toog was too strong. He didn't even wait, just pulled Kirk right up to the edge of the roof, then grabbed him with both hands and lifted him off his feet …

And I thought that was it.

I really thought he was going to throw Kirk off.

And maybe he would have.

But just as he lifted him up, the door to the roof slammed open, and we all turned round to see who it was.

It was Della. She was breathing heavily, and her face was sickly white. She was clutching a hand to her chest.

"Della!" cried Marcus. "What the hell …? I *told* you to stay at home."

"I was worried," she gasped. She looked over at me. "I just wanted to—"

Thump.

The sudden sound came from behind me. I turned round and saw Toog crashing to the ground. We'd all taken our eyes off Kirk for a moment. And while we weren't watching him, he'd head-butted Toog and knocked him out. And now Kirk was going after Marcus.

"Marcus!" I yelled.

But I was too late. As Marcus turned round, Kirk flashed past me and laid Marcus out with a brutal punch to the head. I was too shocked to move. All I could do was stand there and watch as Kirk kicked Marcus in the head. Then he turned round and started running for the door.

Della was too shocked to move, too. She was still standing in front of the door. Just standing there, staring at Kirk. He was running right at her.

"Della!" I shouted. "Move! Get out of the way!"

When she heard me screech at her like that, she moved – a fearful step to one side. But it didn't do her any good. Because Kirk wasn't running for the door, after all – he was running for her. I watched in horror as he swerved to one side and grabbed her by the hand. Then he started dragging her back across the roof towards me.

I looked around. Marcus was still out of it, groaning quietly on the ground, and Toog was just lying there like a fallen tree. I looked back at Kirk and Della.

Della was grasping her chest. She could hardly breathe.

Kirk was grinning at me.

"Leave her alone," I told him. "She's got nothing to do with this."

His grin got even bigger.

"She's sick," I said. "She's got a bad heart."

"Yeah? That's a shame."

He jerked her hand. She stumbled and yelped. He dragged her to her feet and put his arm round her neck, then pushed her over to the edge of the roof. His eyes were shining with madness now. He was crazy. Grinning like a lunatic.

"Fresh air," he shouted at me. "That's what you need when you're sick – plenty of fresh air." He leaned out over the edge and looked down, forcing Della to look down, too. She screamed. Kirk smiled madly at her, then looked at me. "How d'you think it feels?" he yelled. "You know, when you're falling … plunging down to the ground – how d'you think it feels? D'you think you *think* about anything? What d'you think, Delgado? What would *you* think about?"

I didn't say anything. There wasn't anything to say. I kept my eyes fixed on Della. She was trembling and shaking in

Kirk's grip, but I could see she was still in control of herself.

Kirk laughed. "Hey, d'you know what Tyrell said when I stabbed him? D'you know what he said? He said I was making a big mistake. Can you *believe* that? He's lying there with a knife in his guts, and he says *I'm* making a big mistake."

Della winked at me.

What was she trying to tell me?

"See," said Kirk, "the trouble with Tyrell was—"

Della suddenly gasped, a loud painful gasp. Then she grabbed at her chest and went limp. Kirk didn't know what to do next. He looked down at Della, slumped in his arms. Just for one moment he stepped back from her so as to hold her a different way. That was what Della was waiting for. As soon as she felt Kirk's arm relax, she threw back her head and nutted him in the face. Then she lifted her foot up and raked her boot down his shin. As Kirk swore and staggered back, Della spun out of his grip and quickly backed away from him. I reached out and pulled her towards me. Kirk lunged after her, trying to grab her arm, but his foot slipped and he missed. And as he fell over, I shoved him away.

And he lost his balance.

Toppled sideways.

Over the edge of the roof.

I don't know *why* I lunged after him and grabbed his hand – I just did. I wasn't thinking about it. I just saw him going over the edge, and the next thing I knew I was lying face down on the roof, with my head over the edge, and Kirk was swinging in my hand below me.

His face peered up at me – petrified, sick, shocked.

His body was twisting in the air.

"Keep still," I told him. I gritted my teeth. "Just hold on ..."

He was heavy.

Twenty-three floors below, I could see crowds of people looking up, their tiny faces lit up in the eerie flashing blue lights from the police cars.

It was a long way down.

"Don't let go," Kirk whimpered. "Please ... don't drop me ..."

I looked at him. I felt strangely calm now. My arm was being pulled out of its socket, and my hand was throbbing, but my head was as clear as a bell.

"Why did you set me up?" I said.

"What?" he hissed.

"I can't hold on for ever," I told him. "The quicker you tell me—"

"All right, all *right*," he spluttered. "It was nothing, OK? I just needed someone to take the heat, take the blame for killing Jones. I set you up, OK? I admit it. Now pull me up, *please* ..."

"Why me?" I said. "Why choose me?"

"No *reason*," he spat. "I just heard about you, that's all. You know – the private detective kid. You were easy to set up, that's all it was. You were easy."

He looked down. His eyes rolled with fear.

I could feel his hand slipping out of mine.

I put my other hand into my pocket and took out Betty's phone. I looked at the display. The line was still open.

I put the phone to my ear. "Did you get all that?"

"This is the emergency services," a voice said. "Who is this please?"

"My name's Johnny Delgado. I'm on the roof of the North Tower on the William B. Foster estate. Is this call being recorded?"

"Please stay where you are. The police are on their way. Is anybody injured, Johnny? It sounded like—"

I held the phone out to Kirk. "It's been on since you got here," I told him. "They heard everything."

"Please," he begged. "Help me ..."

"One more thing," I said.

"No ..."

"Who killed my dad?"

He shook his head. "I don't know. I was just joking about him ... the letter was a fake. I don't know anything. Please ... I don't *know* ..."

"Name," I said. "Give me a name."

"I *can't* ..."

He was crying now. Tears streaming down his face.

"You're slipping, Lee," I told him. "I can't hold on. Last chance ... give me a name."

He stared up at me, his eyes were bulging. His lips shut tight.

Then finally he blurted out a name.

Chapter 11
Working On It

It took a little while, and lots of explaining, but everything turned out all right in the end.

I didn't drop Kirk off the roof. I wasn't strong enough to haul him back up, but I managed to hang on to him until Marcus and Toog were able to give me a hand, and then it was easy. Once we'd got him back on the roof, Toog was all for giving him a good kicking. But, luckily for Kirk, the police arrived just in time. They arrested the lot of us and took us all down to the station.

Six hours later, I was home and free. Thanks to the 999 call I'd made on the roof, the police had heard everything Kirk had said. They'd heard him admit to Tyrell Jones's murder, and they'd heard him admit he'd set me up. It wasn't enough to *prove* I was innocent, but it was enough for them to let me go.

By Monday morning, the police had charged Kirk with the murder of Tyrell Jones. The tall black kid and the guy with the face like a pizza were both arrested and charged with planning to commit murder. Carly and Bex were taken in to the police station for questioning and arrested for helping Kirk. They were later released on bail.

Marcus and Toog were both released without charge.

As far as I know, Della is fine. She's still not great, but I think she's doing OK. Her mum has banned me from seeing her now, as she thinks I'm bad for her heart, so we haven't had a chance to meet up for a while. But I'm working on it.

And the name? The name that Kirk blurted out as he was hanging over the edge of the roof ... the name of the man who killed my dad? Well, I'm working on that, too. The name Kirk gave me was Taylor – Jack Taylor. So far, all I've managed to find out about him is that he used to be my dad's boss, and that soon after my dad died he left the police and set up his own private detective agency.

It's not much to go on, I know.

But, like I said, I'm working on it.

I'll let you know how I get on.

Johnny's back –
and this time it's personal ...

Johnny Delgado:

Like Father, Like Son

A gang war is about to blow Johnny's estate apart. But Johnny's got problems of his own.

1. Find out who killed his father

2. Find out why

3. Get revenge

The truth is out there. Johnny just needs to kick down a few doors to get to it ...

Barrington Stoke would like to thank all its readers for commenting on the manuscript before publication and in particular:

Ann Bradwell

Staci-Leigh Clark

Alex Conn

Heather Forsyth

Dale Glover

Judi Gornall

Chris Hinkins

Heather Holmyard

James Hufford

Sonny Medler

George Parker

Morag René

Damien Richards

Henry Richardson

Hollie Sadler

Jake Sayers

Jamie Skilton

Harvey Smith

Tony Tingley

Stephen Westlake

Become a Consultant!

Would you like to give us feedback on our titles before they are published? Contact us at the email address below – we'd love to hear from you!

info@barringtonstoke.co.uk
www.barringtonstoke.co.uk